Pippo Gets Lost

PIPPO

HELEN OXENBURY

ALADDIN BOOKS
Macmillan Publishing Company • New York

Sometimes Pippo gets
lost and I have to
look for him.

I asked Mommy if she'd seen
Pippo, and she said I should
look in my toy-chest again. Pippo
wasn't there, but I found his scarf.

Daddy said, "Did you look
under your bed?" But all I
found there was Pippo's hat.

I got really worried
about Pippo and
thought I might
never see him again.

Mommy said that Pippo couldn't
be far away and said that we should
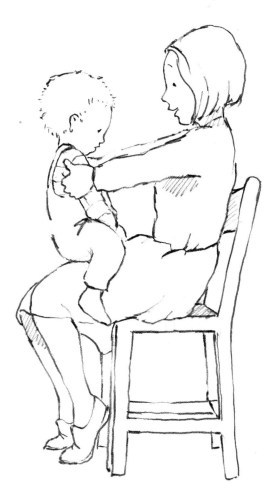
look in the living
room. And that's
where he was all
the time, in the
bookcase.

I told Pippo to tell me
before he goes away
next time.